This books belongs to

....

BAH HUMBUG.

NO MORE  CARROTS!

RED-NOSE REINDEER UNION

I'M WITH DANCER →

OVERTIME? THAT'S RUDE-DOLPH.

FELIZ NAVI-DON'T

I'M WITH PRANCER

Jingle all the way, YOURSELF!

OH DEER

ALL I WANT FOR CHRISTMAS IS A DAY OFF.

Written by Holly Lansley.
Illustrated by Clare Fennell.

Reindeer on STRIKE!

Clare Fennell • Holly Lansley

make
believe
ideas

There's just **one** day 'til Christmas; the toys are almost done.
Your list has been checked twenty times, maybe **twenty-one**!
Your sleigh's out of the garage; the snow forecast is fine;
your suit is being dry-cleaned –
EVERYTHING'S on TIME!

...are saying they're on STRIKE!

NORTH

REINDEER GO ON STRIKE!

TURN TO PAGE 25 FOR AN EXCLUSIVE INTERVIEW WITH BLITZEN.

POLE PRESS

DECEMBER 24TH / NORTH POLE / 2 CANDY CANES

Oh deer!
I'm **stuffed** like turkey
if I don't have a sleigh.
Come on, Mike, we have to think
and find **another** way.

Thank you so much,
everyone!
You've really **saved** the day.
Which makes me think –
before we leave,
there's something I should say . . .

The End

Dream team!

Too much gingerbread?

Dancer's first ballet performance

Sleigh-racing champs

Friends forever

Christmas Island break

Best Head Elf